When love comes to me and says
What do you know, I say This girl, this boy.

— Sharon Olds, from "Looking at Them Asleep"

To those who, with their love and dreaming,
make this world more livable for all.
– af & ag

www.enchantedlion.com
First published in 2021 by Enchanted Lion Books,
248 Creamer Street, Studio 4, Brooklyn, NY 11231

Book design by Eugenia Mello | Title Lettering by Ohara Hale

ISBN 978-1-59270-321-0

A CIP record is on file with the Library of Congress

Printed in Italy by Società Editoriale Grafiche AZ
First Edition

What Do You Know?

Written by Aracelis Girmay & Ariana Fields
Illustrated by Ariana Fields

Enchanted Lion Books
NEW YORK

When love comes to the well and asks,
What do you know,
it says,
I know thirst, I know abundance.

I know depth, I know darkness.

When love comes to the farmers and asks,
What do you know,
he says,

I know the colors of the earth's flat face.

She says, *I know work and weather*
and the hands of the sun and the rain.

When love comes to the honey bees and asks,
What do you know,
they say,
We know the bright heads of the yarrow and the hyssop
and the ruffles of the horsemint flowers.

And we know the hexagon and the color gold.

We know the black bear's hunger for honey.

When love comes to the historian and asks,
What do you know,
she says,
I know history speaks when we listen
for the quietest stories among the stories.

When love comes to the forest and asks,
What do you know,
it says,
I know the color green and the color brown
and the billion creatures and creature sounds.

I know the call of the monkey, the breath of the bear,
the red of the ants and the shade's dark gown.

And I know the musk we make when the rain comes down.

When love comes to the ash and asks,
What do you know,
the ash says, *I know the secrets between the volcano and the sky.*

It says, *I know wandering,*

and I know the language of fire.

When love comes to the rock and asks,
What do you know,
the rock says,
I know the force of the water and the force of the wind.

And I know that change is possible, even if it takes a million years.

When love comes to the goats and asks,
What do you know,
they say,

We know the face of the cliff,
and we know the balance of our hooves
on the jagged edges.

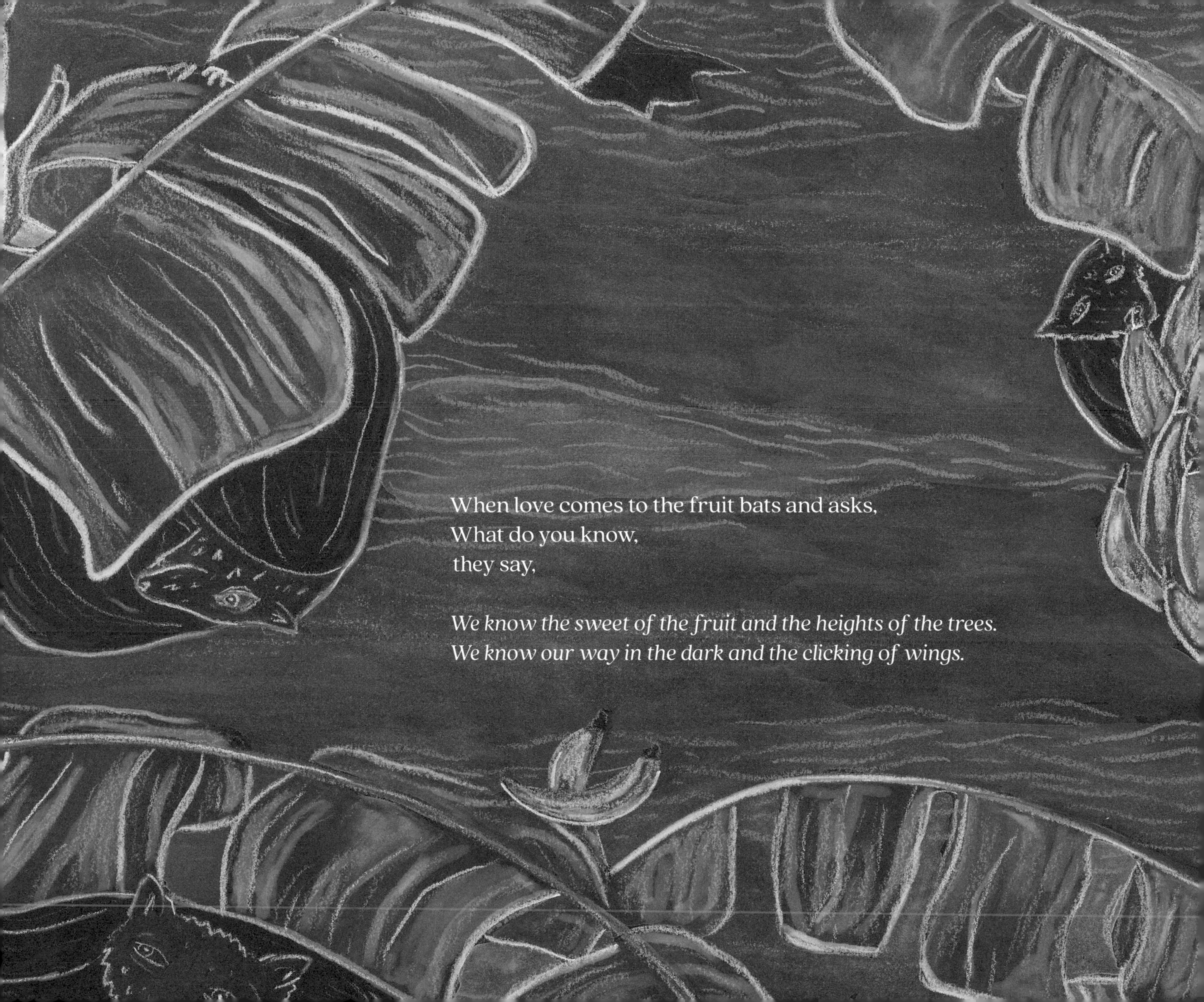

When love comes to the fruit bats and asks,
What do you know,
they say,

We know the sweet of the fruit and the heights of the trees.
We know our way in the dark and the clicking of wings.

When love comes to the Seven Sisters and asks,
What do you know,
they say,
We know the silence of outer space
and the vastness of the deep, dark night.

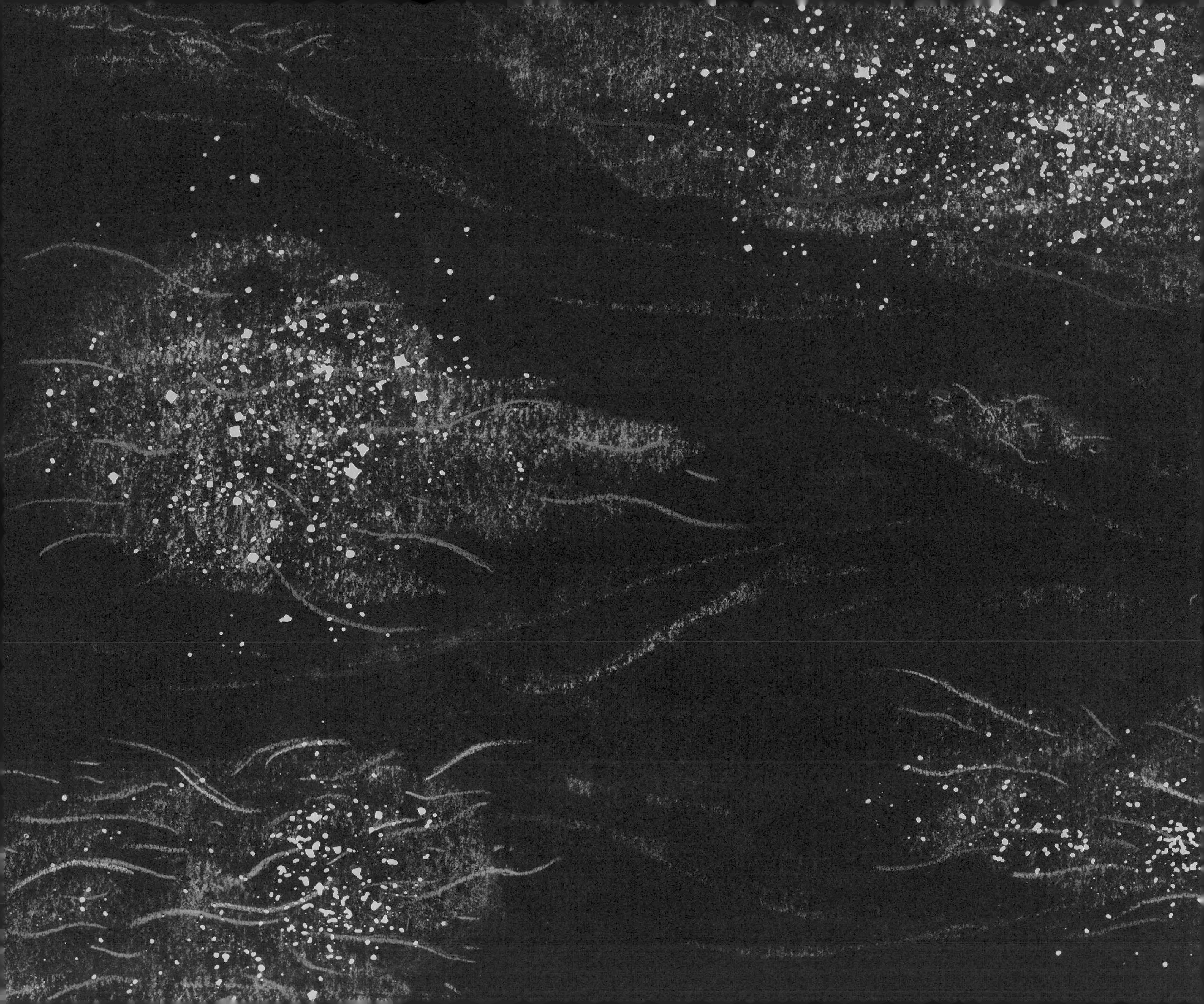

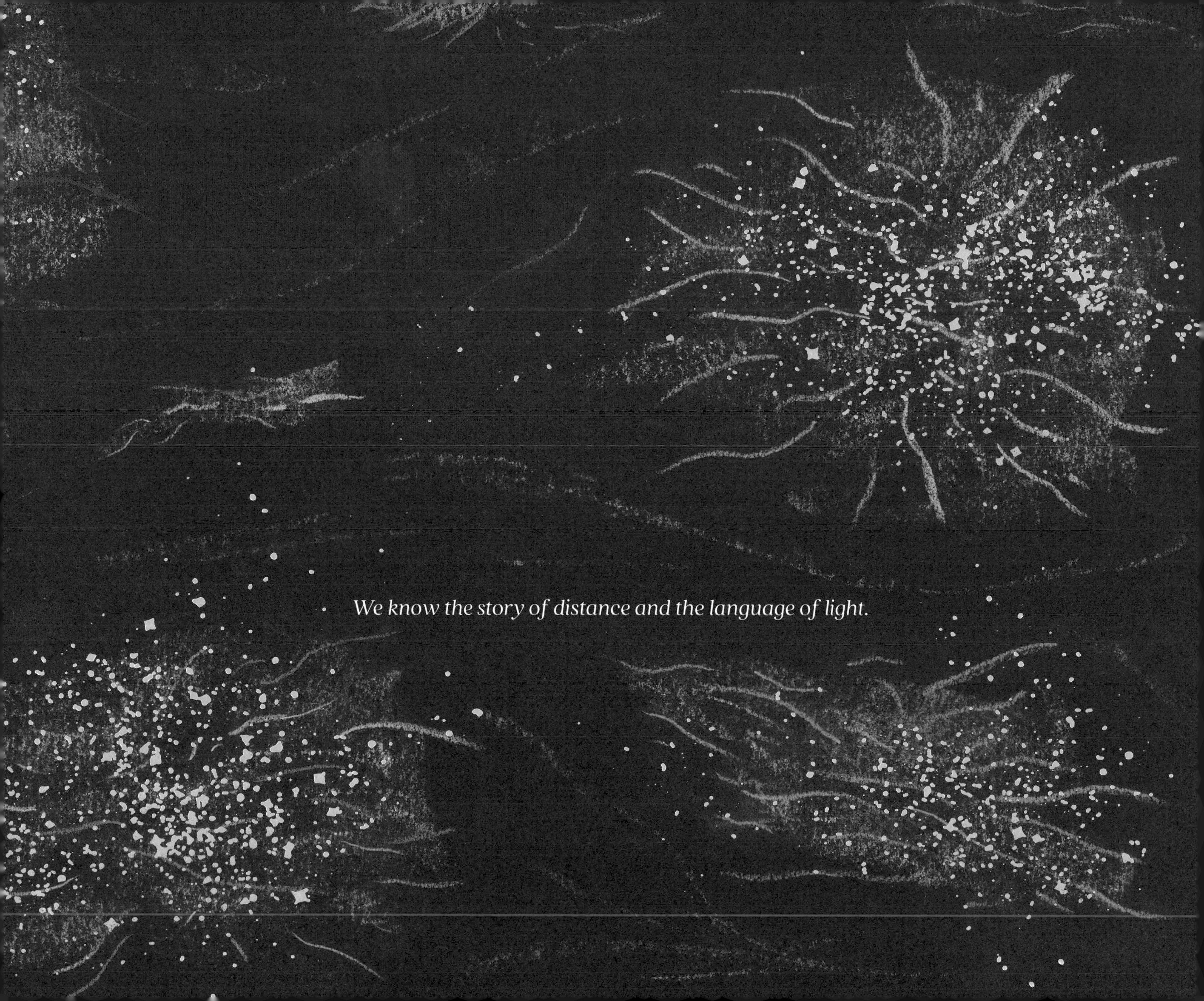

We know the story of distance and the language of light.

When love comes to courage and asks,
What do you know,
courage says,
I know speaking, even though I am afraid,
and I know the daily work of keeping on.

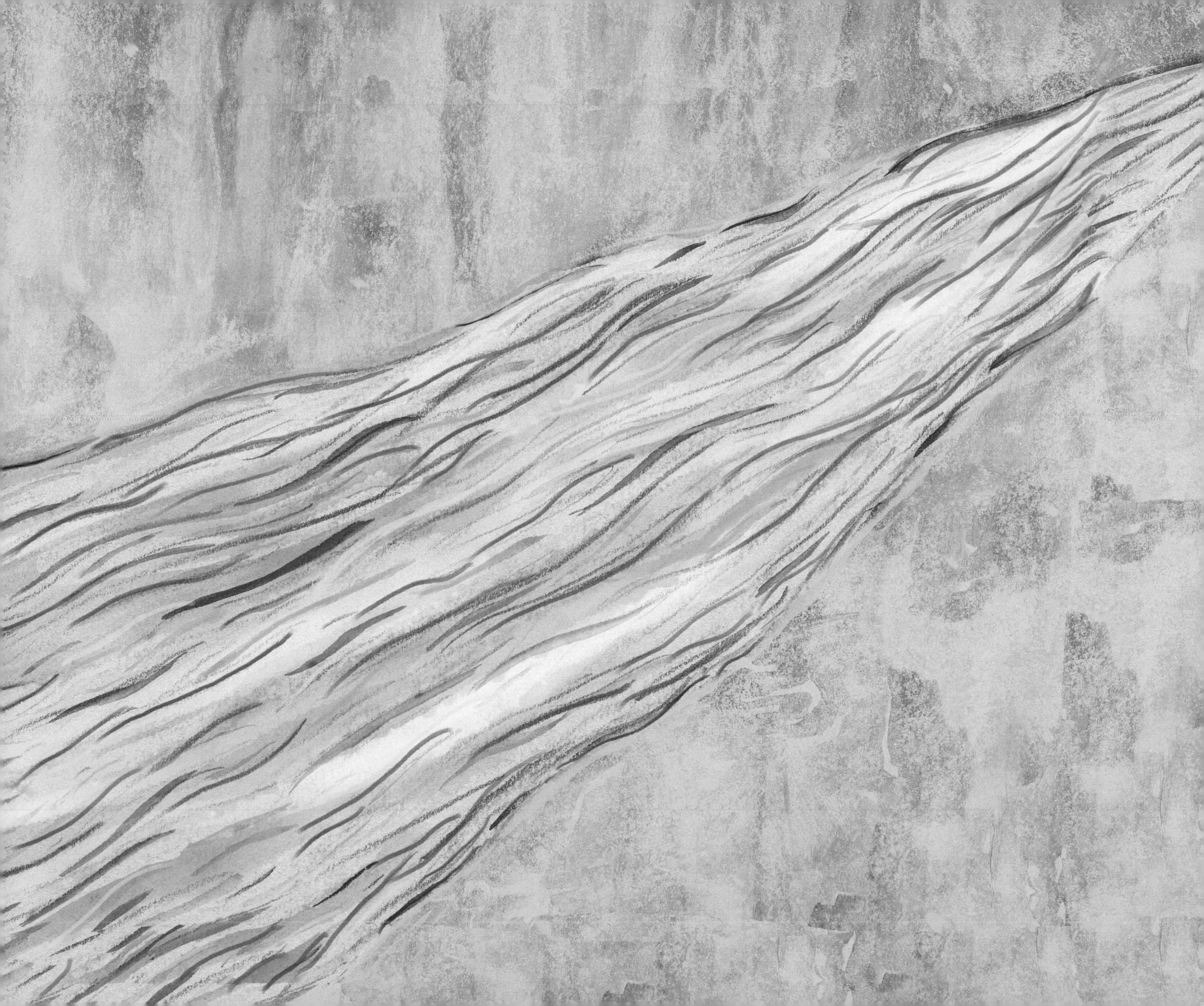

When love comes to the seafarer and asks,
What do you know,
she says,

I know the breath of the ocean and the eye of the whale.
I know the strength of my muscles as they pull the rope.

And I know that star

and that star.

When love comes to the land and asks,
What do you know,
the land says, *I know the joy of going on and on and on.*

And I know the laughter of children who run below the birds,
and the heels and toes of the elders who planted the seeds.

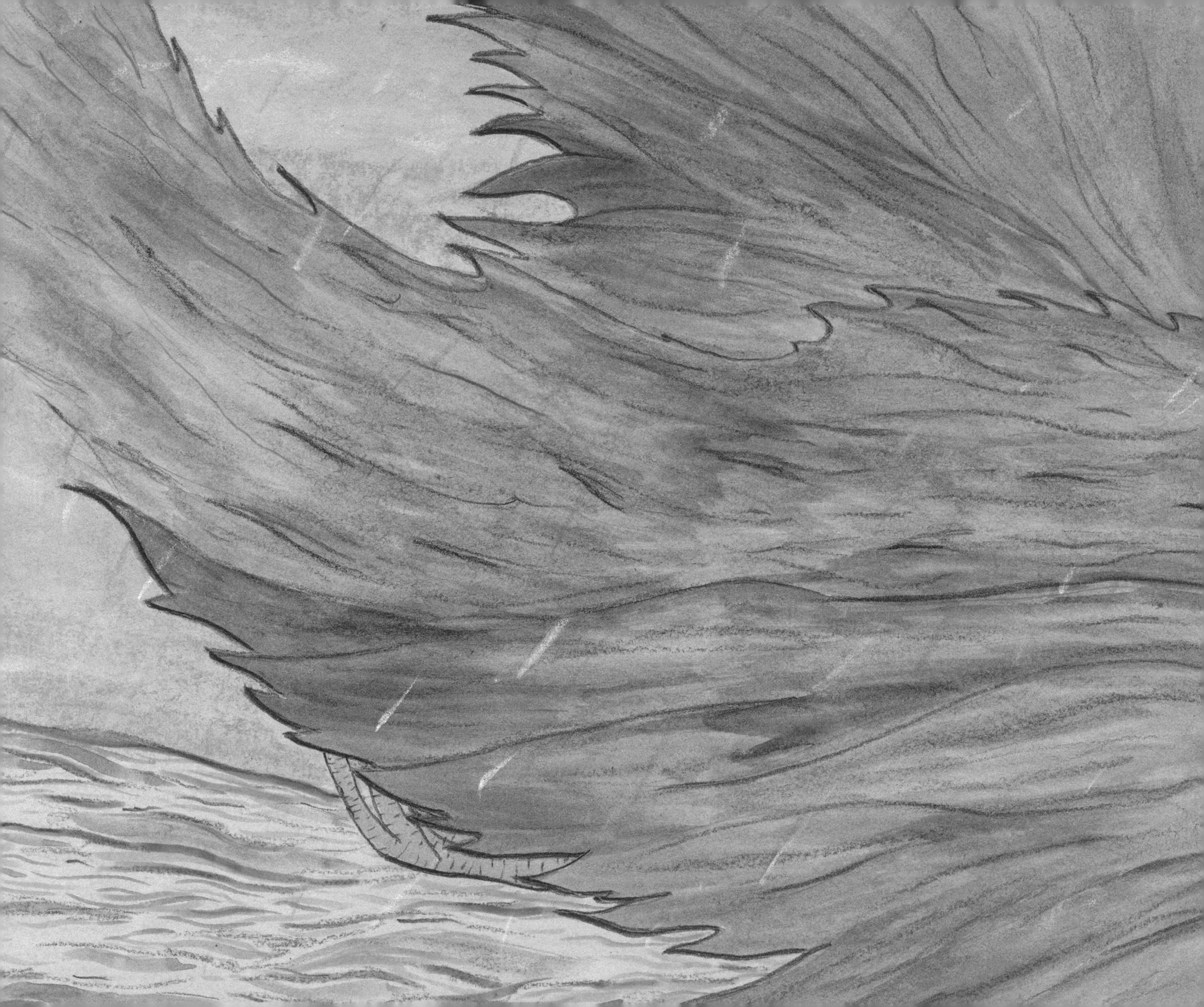

I know the ancestors and their ancestor dreams,
the hoping song that is brown and the hoping song that is green.

Authors' Note

We are sisters, so our collaboration begins there—across the years and walks and nights and tables. But it was in 2015 that we first started taking notes toward the text that would become this book. We were writing something with Ara's son, Ariana's nephew, newly born, in mind. The text grew out of a stirring to make something for very young people—a refuge, an encouragement, an insistence on wonder and wonder anywhere. We wrote the text together, Ariana made some drawings, and then we put it aside, as though planting a yam into the earth, allowing it its quiet and growth and sleep. Two years later we unearthed it to see what it might be. We sent it off to Enchanted Lion. They said yes.

And so began this new iteration of our collaboration. With hands, pencils, watercolor, Ariana continued to work on the images. We met in winter, we met in spring, and then another winter. We had a thousand conversations, all the while feeling emboldened by beauty, this chance to make an offering toward young people—Here, Gone, Coming.